JF HUG.

The Copper Crust

The Copper Crust

Mair Wynn Hughes

Illustrations by
Brett Breckon

PONT BOOKS

First impression—1992

ISBN 0 86383 831 6

© Mair Wynn Hughes

This novel was commissioned by the Welsh Arts Council and was first published in 1989 in Welsh as *Caleb,* under the auspices of the WJEC's Welsh Readers Scheme as part of the Welsh History Project.

This book is published with the support of the Welsh Arts Council.

*Printed by J. D. Lewis & Sons, Ltd.,
Gomer Press, Llandysul, Dyfed, Wales.*

1

'Wait for me, Caleb,' wailed Catrin. 'Wait for me.'

Her lower lip trembled as she fought against the tears.

'I'm t-tired,' she sobbed as the tears spilled down her dusty face.

Caleb sighed. Catrin was only little, hardly more than a baby, really. But it didn't matter how young you were, you still had to work. He sighed again. He was tired too. His legs ached, and the pain stabbed at his back, making every step an effort. He watched Meri and Siôn, his brother and sister, trudging ahead. They liked gleaning. That was because they were older and stronger and had never suffered from the fever. Caleb wished that he was strong and healthy too. Perhaps he would be— one day.

He turned, hunching his shoulders, and waited for Catrin.

'We're nearly home,' he called encouragingly. 'Only a little further, Catrin.'

He stretched his back painfully. The pain was worse because he'd been bent over double in the cornfield gleaning all day. It was work that he hated. He'd had to walk and walk with bent body picking the few ears of corn and straw that the farmer had left behind after the harvest.

There were only a few at best, but today they'd gleaned less than usual. Weeks of rain had spoilt most of the harvest, and the farmer had left very little for the gleaners.

Ahead of him Siôn had stopped.

'Come on. Don't be a baby, Catrin,' he shouted.

Catrin's eyes filled with tears again. Then she threw her small bundle of straw to the ground and sat determinedly on the grass.

'Now look what you've done,' scolded Meri. 'You know we should carry every scrap home, and not waste a single ear.'

'She's only little,' said Caleb.

He sat beside Catrin. Oh! How he wished that he could sit there without moving until the pain in his back was just a little better, and how he wished that the cottage was a little nearer.

'She's only four,' he said again. 'And besides, I'm tired too.'

'Well, I'm not stopping,' said Siôn. 'I'm hungry. Maybe we'll have swede for supper.'

Suddenly, the four felt very hungry. They'd had nothing but a few blackberries since their bowl of bread and milk at breakfast—and it had been a very small bowl of bread and milk too.

Caleb's stomach rumbled painfully. He rose slowly to his feet and stretched a hand to help his sister.

'Come on, Catrin,' he said. 'I'll hold your hand, and we'll walk together.'

'She should learn to work like everybody else,' grumbled Meri. 'What's the point of complaining? Everybody works, and everybody gets tired.'

She walked ahead with Siôn. Caleb and Catrin followed slowly, holding hands.

'Will you carry me?' Catrin asked hopefully. 'Just for a little way. Please, Caleb?'

Caleb shook his head. How could he carry Catrin when he could hardly walk himself.

'Don't pester Caleb,' ordered Siôn. 'You know he's been ill with the fever.'

'Will you carry me then?' asked Catrin. 'Just a little way?'

But Siôn shook his head and quickened his step so as to catch up with Meri.

'You're old enough to walk,' he called over his shoulder.

Catrin started to cry as Caleb squeezed her hand comfortingly.

'We'll walk very slowly, Catrin,' he promised. 'Then you won't feel so tired.'

Soon Meri and Siôn had vanished in the distance. Caleb looked after them longingly. How he wished that he was nearer home. He closed his eyes for a moment and tried to imagine himself reaching the cottage. There would be smoke curling lazily from the open chimney place. He knew the door would be open and the smell of swede cooking would tickle his nose as he stepped over the threshold.

Mam would be so glad to see him. She would fuss over him and lead him to the little three-legged stool by the fire. She would worry that he had worked too long in the field, and maybe rub his back because she'd know how badly it ached.

And then she'd fetch a bowl of cooked swede for him to eat, and if he was lucky, there would be a small dab of butter on top, and maybe, a crust of bread for him to bite into. His stomach rumbled loudly as he imagined the taste of hot swede and butter on his tongue.

He came back to reality with a bump. There was a blister on his heel . . . on both heels. It was because of the boots. They had belonged to William, his big brother. Then to Siôn . . . and to Meri . . . and now to him. And if they lasted long enough, they would belong to Catrin too. They all wore old boots because there wasn't any money to buy new ones. The blisters pinched again as he limped on.

At last, they reached the gate on top of the hill.

9

'Look Catrin,' said Caleb pointing. 'There's our cottage. We won't be long now.'

How comforting the cottage looked with its uneven stone walls and thatched roof. But it was still a long way off.

'Through the gate . . . across the sheepwalk . . . and down the hill. *Then*, we'll be home. Mam will be waiting, and so will our supper, Catrin. Look, Meri and Siôn are almost there!'

His stomach gnawed with hunger as he thought again of the swede and the butter that would, hopefully, be waiting. Maybe there would be *two* swedes. Enough for a second bowlful. He wouldn't care if there wasn't any butter then. He would feel warm and full and tired all at once.

'Come on, Catrin . . .' he began.

Then he stopped suddenly as he heard the sound of hooves. Caleb turned swiftly. A horseman was riding towards them.

'Open the gate, boy,' he called briskly.

'Yes, sir. At once, sir,' replied Caleb.

He pulled and pushed at the heavy gate and wondered who the rich looking horseman could be. He looked so smart in his dark coat and his high crowned hat, and in the black boots that reached up to his knees. I could see my face in the shine on those boots, thought Caleb dreamily.

The horseman smiled down at him and reached into his pocket.

'Here,' he said. 'Pennies for opening the gate.'

Caleb forgot about the stabbing pain in his back and the tiredness in his legs as he scrambled for the pennies.

'*Two* pennies, Catrin,' he called excitedly. 'One for you, and one for me. He was a kind man, wasn't he? And won't Mam be pleased!'

He wanted to run and run all the way to the cottage. *Two pennies!* That was a fortune. With two pennies they could afford a proper meal tomorrow, with lots of vegetables. A soup made with carrots and onions and swede and potatoes. No meat, of course. You needed more than two pennies to buy meat.

Caleb stared longingly after the horseman as he grew smaller and smaller in the distance. Sometimes, he imagined himself with a father exactly like the stranger. A rich, rich father, who could afford to give him plenty of food and proper clothing. He would have a nice fat pony of his own to ride, and he would wear a jacket and breeches and a cap on his head.

'That was a nice horse, wasn't it, Catrin?' he said.

But Catrin was too tired to listen.

'I want to go home, Caleb,' she sobbed.

'Yes,' said Caleb.

But his eyes were on the horseman disappearing in the distance.

'Some day, I'll work with horses like that,' he promised. 'When I'm grown up, Catrin. Then I shall have *plenty* of money. I'll buy lots and lots of food for us all. Swede and potatoes and buttermilk, flour to make bread with, and herring to smoke above the fire. Won't that be fine, Catrin?'

But Catrin was too tired to answer.

Caleb walked dreamily on. He loved horses, especially Twm, the old carthorse that grazed behind the cottage. He would steal away sometimes to feed him the very last piece of bread from his pocket.

Twm always knew he was coming. He would neigh in welcome and stretch his soft lips towards the pocket. Caleb smiled to himself as he remembered how warm and silky Twm's coat was, and how he, Caleb, loved to bury his face in his neck and smell the sweetish comforting smell that was a part of his beloved friend.

At last, they arrived at the cottage. Caleb hoped that there was some supper left. But, of course, Mam would never let Meri and Siôn eat it all. What there was, was always shared equally.

'Mam! Mam!' he shouted from the doorway. 'Look what we were given. *Two pennies!* By a kind man on a horse. He must have been rich, Mam. And kind too. He smiled at us. But, oh, he was so grand in his breeches and tall hat, Mam, . . . and his horse was big and strong, but lively too . . .

'You and your horses,' Mam said, smiling tiredly.

She pushed the wisp of greying hair behind her ears, and pulled her thin shawl tighter across her shoulders. She looked at the two pennies that Caleb had given her.

'Yes . . . they will be a help,' she sighed. 'And, yes, he was a kind man, Caleb.'

Then she looked at the straw bundle that he carried.

'How much corn did you get?'

'Only this much, Mam,' said Caleb.

'And I got some too,' said Catrin showing her tiny bundle.

Mam looked pale and tired, and was suddenly on the verge of tears.

'So little,' she said to herself. 'So very very little to feed us all.'

Caleb was so hungry that he couldn't stay silent any longer.

'Is there swede for supper?' he asked eagerly. 'And butter, maybe?'

That same expression was on his Mam's face again. Pale and tired and careworn.

'And how are we to get butter?' she asked quietly. 'We must eat what we can get, and be thankful.'

But Caleb didn't feel thankful. He felt hungry and tired and disappointed and angry all at the same time. Why did some people have warm houses and plenty of food to fill their bellies, while others were hungry and cold and aching from the fever like he was?

He watched Mam remove the blackened saucepan from the fire, and he watched her spoon a small portion into each bowl. She put them on the rough wooden table and placed a piece of bread by each one.

'That's all I have,' she said. 'Eat it all.'

Eat it all? Of course, they'd eat it all! And another bowlful besides. But there wasn't any more.

'But, Mam, I'm still hungry,' sobbed Catrin.

They ate quietly. Caleb watched Mam. She looked thin and pale. He suddenly felt afraid. Had she eaten any of the swede? Perhaps she'd given them more, and gone without herself. People became ill and died when they didn't eat. He wished Mam would fill a bowl for herself, and join them at the wooden table. But she never did, he realised now. He worried again.

He relaxed when he heard footsteps outside. Da and William, his elder brother had arrived.

14

He sighed happily. Da would take care of them all. Of course, he would.

He turned as the door opened. Maybe Da had some extra food for them. Potatoes, or maybe buttermilk, that the farmer had given him at the end of a long working day. Da was a good worker. And William, too.

But Da had nothing. Caleb watched him walk heavily to the bench by the fire. Mam and Da looked at each other for a long moment. Then Da shook his head wearily and stared into the fire without saying a word.

Caleb's heart jumped painfully. He knew that something was wrong. The others knew too. They stopped eating and stared at Da. They waited for him to say something. Anything. But the silence stretched and stretched, and still Da stared into the fire.

At last, Mam laid a hand on his shoulder.

'What is it, John?' she asked quietly.

Da sighed heavily.

'There's no more work to be had,' he said. 'Not for me, or for William. This is our last wage.'

The sound of Mam's sudden gasp filled the cottage.

'No more work? Oh, John! How will we manage?'

Her voice was fearful.

'We'll have to leave here, and start begging like so many others,' replied Da sadly.

Beg? The children looked at each other. The same fear was in all their eyes. How could they become beggars wandering from place to place with no cottage to sleep in at night, and no fire to warm their shivering bodies? And winter was nearly here.

'I don't want to beg,' wailed Catrin throwing herself at Mam. 'Say we can stay. Say we can stay.'

Mam put her arms around Catrin and held her tight.

'Shush, Catrin fach,' she said. 'Shush. Da will take care of us.'

But her hands were shaking.

'There is another way,' said Da suddenly. 'We must go to Amlwch like my brother Tomos. There's plenty of work there for us all.'

'But . . .' said Mam. 'But . . .' she said again.

Then she looked at Da, and her shoulders slumped. Amlwch was better than being beggars. Of course it was.

'Yes, John. We'll go tomorrow,' she said.

2

It was early morning. Caleb lay awake on the chaff mattress that he shared with his

16

brothers and sisters. He was warm and cosy amongst the tangle of arms and legs and limp bodies around him, but he had been awake for hours.

He had been awake for most of the night. He was afraid of the 'tomorrow' that would see them leaving the cottage for ever, and setting off for Amlwch. And now that 'tomorrow' had finally arrived. Already he could make out the familiar outlines of things inside the cottage. The wooden table and the bench, the old iron saucepan and the three-legged stool. But today, they were all jumbled together ready for the journey.

Caleb stared into the brightening darkness. He stared at the old familiar things that he awoke to every morning. He stared at the thatched roof through which water dripped when it was raining; he stared at the dirt floor flattened to a hard surface by all the feet that had trodden it, and he stared at the uneven walls that had lumps of mud mixed with straw between the stones to keep out the wind and rain.

His eyes filled with tears. This was *home*. He loved the fields and the sheepwalk. He loved the feel of the wind on his face and the smell of the gorse in full bloom, and above all, he loved Twm. What would Twm do without him? There would be nobody to take him a stealthy

17

crust or to rub his coat with a tuft of grass until it shone. Caleb blinked back the tears. Someday he would return. Someday . . . when he'd grown tall and strong.

People could earn a good wage at Amlwch. He'd heard Da say so. They would have plenty of money to feed them all. There would be work for Da and William. For Meri and Siôn, and, maybe, even for him. And there was a doctor in Amlwch. Da had said that too. A doctor who would give him special medicine to cure his aching back. Then he would be able to work like the others.

Caleb sighed to himself as he burrowed deeper into the arms and legs and sleeping bodies around him. He wanted to be big and strong more than anything in the world. And, someday, he wanted to work with horses. Any sort of horses would do.

Caleb thought of Twm again. He rose stealthily so as not to disturb the others. He couldn't leave home without saying goodbye to Twm, could he? He shivered in the damp morning air. The fire on the hearth was a heap of cold ashes, and it had started to rain outside. He could hear it pattering loudly on the thatched roof and dripping faster and faster onto the dirt floor in the corner. He moved quietly towards the door.

'Caleb? Are you ill?' whispered Mam.

Then Da awoke.

'It's time we all got up,' he said gruffly.

Caleb swallowed. Da would be angry because he wanted to visit Twm.

'Where were you going, Caleb?' Mam asked.

'To see Twm,' answered Caleb.

The anger spread on Da's face.

'There's no time for such silliness,' he said. 'We must start soon. We have a long way to go, and pushing a loaded cart is heavy work.'

But Mam smiled at Caleb.

'Let him be, John,' she said. 'Twm is his friend . . . and you know Caleb has been ill.'

Da still looked angry, but he shrugged as he turned away to load the cart for the journey.

'Hurry up, then,' he ordered. 'We'll be off as soon as Mam has cut a few slices of bread for breakfast.'

'Put a sack over your shoulders . . . *and hurry back*,' called Mam as Caleb opened the door.

The rain was heavy on his face as he climbed the steep slope behind the cottage. He wished that he could run up the slope as Siôn did. But he couldn't. His back ached so much.

But he forgot about the ache in his back as soon as he saw Twm. He was tethered amongst the gorse as usual. He whinnied loudly when he saw Caleb.

Caleb ran to him and threw his arms around his neck. He smoothed his hand over his wet coat and whispered in his ear.

'Are you glad to see me, Twm?'

Then he shook his head sadly as Twm nuzzled his pocket.

'Nothing for you today, Twm. Not even a tiny crust of bread. And . . . oh, Twm, I'm going away. To Amlwch. But I'll be back someday. Don't forget me, Twm. *Please!*'

Meri called from below.

'Ca . . . leb!'

Caleb gave Twm one last pat.

'I'm coming,' he called.

But he didn't want to go. He turned back and patted Twm again.

'You won't forget me, Twm, will you?' he whispered sadly.

'Ca . . . leb! We're going. *Now.*'

The sack across his shoulders was dripping wet already. But Caleb didn't care. He was sad because he had to leave Twm . . . and his home . . . and all the things that he loved.

He slithered down the slope and pretended that it was rain running down his face, and not tears. But Mam knew. She put a comforting arm around his shoulders and handed him a slice of bread.

'Eat it as you walk,' she said.

But Caleb was too sad to eat anything. He

watched his parents search the cottage one last time, in case they'd left anything useful behind, and he saw them glance at each other before they closed the cottage door. Then Da rested his hand for a long moment on Mam's shoulder, before he turned and grasped the handles of the heavily laden cart.

'Off we go,' he said heartily. 'Help me push, William.'

Caleb swallowed the sudden lump in his throat. Then he offered his hand to Catrin.

'Come on, Catrin,' he said. 'Hold my hand as we walk. And you can share my bread, too.'

3

It was late afternoon and still they were trudging wearily through mud and puddles and the deep ruts in the winding road. The rain streamed down from the heavy black clouds above. It soaked through their protective sacks to trickle coldly down their backs. They were tired and hungry. But there was nowhere to shelter from the cold and the wet.

Caleb lifted one tired foot past the other. His world was one great big ache. And there was no end in sight. Just rain-soaked gorse and brambles, and puddles and mud into which his

feet sank so deep that he thought he could never lift them out again.

Da and William pushed the heavy cart. And when they were tired, everybody else helped. But now they were all tired and discouraged. Why, oh why, did they have to leave home? It was poor and cold and damp, but it had been home.

'I'm tired, Mam,' sobbed Catrin. 'And so h-hungry. Where's Amlwch, Mam?'

'We'll find shelter soon,' comforted Mam. 'Then we'll have a rest and a bite to eat.'

She looked at Caleb.

'Are you tired, Caleb? Does your back hurt?'

Caleb shook his head. He couldn't say a word. If he did, he knew that he would cry like a baby, and then Mam would cry a little herself and worry that he would get another bout of fever here on the open road.

Mam glanced at him again. Then she turned to Da.

'Isn't there anywhere to shelter, John?' she asked anxiously. 'Caleb will be ill if we don't stop soon.'

Da had spotted a farm in the distance.

'Maybe we can shelter there,' he said. 'And, maybe the farmer will give us some butter-milk to drink, too.'

The farm looked small and dilapidated as they drew nearer. There was mud and filth on the stony yard and the house resembled their own rough cottage at home.

A dog rushed to bark at them as they neared the door. It opened and a woman stood there. There was no welcome on her face.

'I have nothing for beggars,' she said angrily. 'Be off, before I set the dog on you.'

Da dropped the cart handles and stretched to his full height proudly.

'We're not beggars, Missus,' he said. 'We have no money to spare, but William and I will work for shelter and a little food for us all.'

The woman looked at them carefully. Then she nodded reluctantly.

'You can stay in the cowshed tonight,' she said. 'And I'll give you bread and buttermilk for cleaning it out. But only for tonight, mind.'

They dropped gratefully on to the warmth of the dry hay in the cowshed. It was heaven to remove the dripping wet sacks and to rub and rub their numbed bodies with tufts of hay until the blood tingled. But there was no rest for Da and William. They had to sweep and scrape the muck from the cowshed and carry it to the midden outside.

When they had finished, they went to the farmhouse door again. They returned with a barley loaf and a can full of buttermilk.

'She will give us more tomorrow,' said Da.

'But we'll have to leave straight away then, even if it's raining.'

Caleb was almost too tired to eat. He chewed the barley crust and drank a little buttermilk. His eyes closed wearily as he snuggled down in the warm dry hay.

But he couldn't stop shivering in his damp clothes. How he wished that they hadn't begun the journey. At home they would have been lying on the familiar chaff mattress now. The dying embers from the fire would be lighting up the dark cottage, and he would be pulling the ragged blanket tighter around his shoulders and drifting off to sleep . . . happy, because he would see Twm again tomorrow.

He closed his eyes and burrowed deeper into the dry tickly hay. He could hear a soft grinding noise as the cattle chewed their cud contentedly. Gradually, it faded further and further into the background. At last, he slept.

4

Da awoke first next morning.

'The rain has stopped,' he said. 'We must journey on at once.'

The family climbed sleepily from the hay.

Meri and Siôn laughed as they picked bits from their hair and clothing.

'You're a hay man,' giggled Meri. 'Be careful or the cows will nibble at you.'

Caleb climbed slowly from the warmth of the hay. He tried to straighten his back and pretend that it wasn't aching.

'I'll take the can and fetch the buttermilk,' said Da.

Caleb knew that Mam was watching him. He suddenly felt angry. Why did she treat him like a little boy? He was older than Catrin, and she didn't worry about her.

But he knew why. It was because he'd had the fever when he was younger, and it was because his Mam knew that the pain in his back was always there.

'Are you all right, Caleb?'

'Yes,' said Caleb shortly.

He hated the same question over and over again. Every day, every week, every month. Ever since he could remember. It wasn't fair. Why couldn't he be big and strong like the others? They didn't care whether it was rain or fine, or whether they worked or rested.

He forced himself to move faster, as if the pain in his back wasn't there. Da would be angry if he knew about the pain. That was because Da didn't believe in spoiling children even though they'd been ill with the fever. Life was hard, said Da. And you had to work, however ill you felt.

Then Da returned with the buttermilk. He looked angry.

'Drink up quickly,' he said. 'That woman says we must leave straight away. There's no welcome for beggars or wanderers, she said.'

'Fancy calling us that,' said Mam shocked.

They pushed the cart from the dirty yard and journeyed on once again.

'We'll reach Amlwch today,' said Da.

They felt better because of his words and because the sun was shining overhead. But pushing the cart through the muddy potholes was still hard work.

Siôn shouted suddenly.

'Look! Blackberries,' he called. 'Lots of them.'

The children ran towards the brambles alongside the track while Mam and Da smiled thankfully.

'Pick as many as you can,' shouted Da holding out an empty can.

The blackberries were soft and squashy between their fingers, and they were maggotty too. But nobody cared. *Anything* was better than pushing a laden cart along the track and feeling hungrier and hungrier as the butter-milk breakfast settled lower and lower in their stomachs.

They ate the blackberries for dinner. The juice ran sweet and purple down their chins as they sat by the track and rested their weary feet.

'Time to go,' said Da as soon as they'd eaten the last juicy berry.

'But I'm still h-hungry,' protested Catrin.

Everybody was still hungry, but they knew that it was no use complaining. They had nothing else to eat.

'There will be plenty of food once we get to Amlwch,' said Da. 'We'll find Tomos, and he will make us welcome.'

They pushed and slithered behind the cart. Soon the countryside began to change. The autumn colours vanished from the hedgerows, and everything began to look wilted and dead. The water in the brook was a strange orange colour, and every time they breathed, a burning feeling caught at their throats. Then they saw Amlwch in the distance.

'Amlwch!' said Mam dubiously, rubbing her streaming eyes.

'Water!' called Catrin excitedly. '*Lots* of water.'

Da smiled.

'That's the sea, Catrin,' he said. Then he turned. 'But look over there. That's Parys Mountain. The copper mountain where we'll all find work. Then we'll have plenty of money to buy food and clothing.'

'Shoes, too?' asked Catrin.

'Shoes, too,' said Da smiling.

But Mam still looked doubtful. Ominous clouds hung over Parys Mountain. Clouds so big and black that they almost covered the sun. They started to cough as the breeze increased suddenly and blew the evil smelling smoke towards them.

'We'll never be able to live in such a place,' said Mam. 'John, we shall all be ill.'

Da looked downcast too. But he tried to smile.

'We have no choice, Esther,' he said.

They walked slowly on. Soon they reached the outskirts of the town. The streets looked small and mean. The cottages stretched in long untidy lines, and there was filth and mud everywhere. Barefooted children ran wildly through the mire.

Suddenly a horde of ragged youngsters surrounded the family.

'A crust, Mister. A crust,' they shouted, hands outstretched. 'Give us a penny to buy bread.'

Their faces were pale and thin looking beneath the dirt, and their tattered clothes were sewn together.

'Oh! The poor little things,' said Mam tearfully. 'John, we were never as poor and hungry as this.'

'A crust. A crust,' they begged again.

'Be off with you,' said Da angrily. 'We have no bread or money.'

Mam was sobbing beneath her breath. She clasped Catrin's hand and hurried her on.

Caleb felt sad. He longed for the fresh air of the country and the feel of the breeze on his face, and he longed for his home and Twm's friendly neigh whenever he visited him.

Caleb tried to tread carefully through the mire, but everywhere was the same. He wrinkled his nose as he trod in some pig manure, and the next moment he jumped wildly out of the way as two hogs rushed by pursued by a crowd of children.

Catrin began to cry.

'I don't like it here, Mam,' she sobbed. 'It's dirty. I want to go home.'

'Shush, Catrin!'

Mam tried to comfort her as she turned to Da.

'Ask somebody, John. Surely they'll know Tomos.'

Da looked about him.

'Stay here with the cart,' he ordered.

He walked towards a man who lounged nearby.

'I'm looking for Tomos Jones,' he said. 'Tomos Jones who works on Parys Mountain.'

The man spat into the gutter.

'Tomos Jones?' he said. 'This place is full of Tomos Joneses.'

Da tried again.

'Tomos is my brother,' he said. 'His wife is called Margaret. They're from Maenaddwyn.'

'Try up the street,' said the man. 'They're nobody I know.'

He spat again. Then he looked at the cart.

'Just arrived?' he asked.

'Yes,' said Da.

But he said it guardedly. There was something shifty in the man's face. Da hurried back to the cart and grasped the handles.

'Hurry, William,' he said under his breath. 'And keep a sharp look out.'

They hurried up the street.

'That man is following us,' said Mam fearfully. 'Will he try to steal our things, John? Will he attack us?'

'He'd better not try,' said Da. 'And besides, we're a family. He wouldn't dare.'

But he remained on his guard. They all felt threatened by the dark open doorways and the people who stood and stared as they walked by.

They hurried forward asking everyone if they knew Tomos and Margaret Jones from Maenaddwyn. By now it was getting dark, and they all felt tired and disheartened. Caleb's back was just one big ache, and Catrin had long since refused to walk another step. Now she rode on the cart, her face tear-stained and her lower lip trembling as she tried to keep back further tears.

Then, when they had almost given up, they found Uncle Tomos and Aunt Margaret. Da knocked on the closed door, and the whole family sighed with relief when it opened. Their Uncle Tomos stood there open-mouthed.

'John!'

'Tomos!'

Children's faces appeared behind the figure in the doorway and Aunt Margaret's voice came from inside.

'Who's there, Tomos?'

Uncle Tomos led them inside. There was hardly room for everybody. Mam and Da, William, Siôn, Meri, Caleb and Catrin, and Uncle Tomos and Aunt Margaret with their *six* children!

'You must stay here with us,' said Aunt Margaret comfortingly as she moved the iron kettle over the fire.

Caleb looked about him. How could they all squeeze into such a small cottage?

'But you have a full house already,' said Mam.

'Tut! A few more won't make any difference,' said Aunt Margaret.

How glad they were to reach shelter at last. Their journey began to seem like a long and terrible dream. But Caleb knew it was no dream. His back ached more than usual.

'Empty the cart,' said Uncle Tomos. 'Amlwch is not a place to leave things lying around.'

Mam nodded nervously.

'A man was following us,' she said. 'We thought he was planning to steal from the cart.'

'There are people to trust, and people not to trust,' said Uncle Tomos gloomily. 'Life is getting harder for us all here at Amlwch.'

They carried everything in. The plank table and the three-legged stool, the saucepans and the big iron kettle were piled into the corner. Then the chaff mattresses and the worn blankets were placed on the dirt floor. When they had finished there was hardly room to breathe.

'Can we find work at Parys Mountain, Tomos?' asked Da. 'We have hardly any money.'

Uncle Tomos shook his head doubtfully.

'There is work,' he said. 'But the wages are not good, and bread is getting more expensive.'

Caleb listened as Uncle Tomos explained

how to find work on the mountain. He explained how to obtain a 'Bargain' in the copper mine, and how you had to join with others to bid for one. Uncle Tomos also said that work there was getting scarce, but that he would take them there tomorrow and explain to the steward that they were good workmen. And maybe, said Uncle Tomos, the children might be lucky and obtain work breaking the ore for the Copper Ladies.

Aunt Margaret smiled.

'I'm one of the Copper Ladies,' she said proudly. 'Meri and Siôn and Caleb can come with me tomorrow to ask for work.'

Mam and Da looked at each other. It had been a good decision to come to Amlwch. Once they got work, then they'd have money to rent a cottage of their own. There would be plenty of food on the table and clothes to wear, and shoes for their feet too.

Caleb lay on the chaff mattress that night and tried to imagine himself breaking ore for the Copper Ladies. What was a Copper Lady? Aunt Margaret was one, but she didn't look any different from his mother. He wanted to ask one of his cousins, but he was too shy. But, of course, he'd find out in the morning, wouldn't he?'

5

Everybody was awake early the following morning.

'There will be no wages until you have worked a full month, of course,' said Uncle Tomos.

Mam looked at Da despairingly.

'A month? But, John, we have no money to buy food or to rent a cottage.'

'Families should always help one another,' said Aunt Margaret. 'You must stay here with us. You can pay us a little at the end of the month.'

Caleb was happy to stay with his Aunt Margaret and Uncle Tomos. But he didn't believe he would ever like Amlwch. It was such a strange, frightening place. He didn't like the people who stared from the doorways without saying anything, and he didn't like the barefooted children who ran about begging. And he *hated* the smoke that seemed to hang over everything.

He watched his cousins as they dressed and ate a hasty breakfast. He hoped they weren't like the children who begged on the street. But how could they be? They worked for the Copper Ladies, didn't they?

He got up slowly. He winced as he pushed his blistered feet into his boots.

'Come on, slowcoach,' said cousin Huw. 'You'll never be ready for work.'

Caleb tried to eat his porridge a little faster.

'What is a Copper Lady?' he asked.

Huw laughed.

'Why, *everybody* knows about Copper Ladies,' he said. 'They're the women who hammer the copper ore, of course. And they get paid a lot for doing it too.'

'How was I to know?' scowled Caleb.

He wished that he was big and strong enough to punch Huw on the nose for making fun of him.

'Don't take any notice of Huw,' whispered one of the girls. 'He thinks he knows everything.

Huw knows about Parys Mountain, thought Caleb to himself. But he doesn't know about horses. And I do. I know how to scratch behind their ears and how to brush their coats until they shine, and I know how soft their mouths are when they nibble a crust.

He began to feel a little better. But only a little. He wished that he was still in far away Maenaddwyn, miles from the choking smell and dust of Amlwch. And he had to look for work today. At the mountain itself.

Everybody ate quickly. Then Aunt Margaret gave them a crust.

'Keep it until your dinner,' she said.

Mam looked at Caleb.

'Are you all right?' she asked. 'Does your back ache?'

'I'm all right,' mumbled Caleb, his face aflame.

Fancy asking that in front of everyone! Now his cousins were laughing at him. Maybe they thought he was a cry-baby.

Well, he wasn't. He could work as well as anyone if he had the chance. See if he couldn't! He scowled at Huw. He'd show them. He'd find work in the copper mine and bring home a good wage. More than they earned, perhaps!

'How old are you?' asked Huw with a sneer on his face.

'I'm ten,' said Caleb.

'You're very small,' said Huw. 'I'm ten, and I'm much bigger than you. Stronger, too.'

Caleb didn't say anything.

'Can you fight?' asked Huw again.

'No,' said Caleb.

'Coward,' said Huw.

Caleb bit his tongue . . . hard! He'd show Huw. He'd show them all.

He watched open-mouthed as his Aunt Margaret prepared for work. How odd she looked . . . but imposing too. He watched as she tied a yellow spotted kerchief over her head until it almost covered her face and neck, and then put a high crowned black hat on top

38

of it. She put an iron glove on her left hand and then reached for a small hammer with her right. She held herself straight and tall, and she looked different, somehow. As if she was a very important worker.

The dawn was breaking as Caleb followed his Aunt and Uncle along the dusty road. Groups of people hurried silently along, huddling in their ragged clothes. Ahead was the Copper Mountain with it's sulphurous chimneys spewing out an acrid cloud which hung over the landscape. Caleb hated it.

6

Caleb didn't find work. The others did, but he didn't. The steward said he was too weak and sickly looking, and that he needed strong healthy children for the ore breaking. He took Siôn and Meri although they were only eight, but he refused Caleb.

He refused others too. Men and women and children were turned away. But that didn't make Caleb feel any better. He felt sad but angry too, because he couldn't earn a proper wage like the rest of the family. Now his cousins would laugh and call him a 'baby' again.

He walked slowly back towards the town. What could he do? He couldn't go back to Mam and Catrin. Mam would only fuss and try to comfort him by pretending he'd find work tomorrow . . . or maybe the day after . . . or next week even.

And he was ashamed. Ashamed of his weak puny body and ashamed of the constant pain in his back and legs.

He kicked a pebble angrily. He couldn't go back. Not without earning a penny. He kicked the pebble again. Much harder this time. The day stretched in front of him. An empty day with nothing for him to do except wander the dirty streets. But he couldn't go home. He walked slowly on.

'Watch where you're going, can't you?' growled a man staggering from a nearby alehouse.

Caleb's heart lurched as he smelled the beery breath. What if the man attacked him? He turned and ran down the street. He ran on and on until he reached another street where rows of little shops stood side by side with neat looking cottages.

Caleb stopped and stared. These were proper homes with clean steps at every front door. And the shops had dark windows full of exciting goods. Caleb smiled suddenly. Surely there would be work for him here. Maybe he could knock at the doors and offer his services. He would offer to do any work for a penny. And rich people had plenty of pennies.

He hesitated at a shop window. Maybe work in a shop would be best. He could sweep the floor and stack the goods. He sniffed as the wonderful smell of leather wafted from the open doorway. It reminded him of Twm.

Caleb squashed his nose against the window and peered in hopefully. He could see reins and saddles, and harness too. He took a deep breath holding the homely comforting smell for as long as he could in his lungs.

He let it out again ... quickly, as the shopkeeper appeared in the doorway. He was waving furiously, and his face was bad tempered underneath his cap.

'Away with you ... beggar boy,' he shouted. 'Away with you!'

Caleb opened his mouth to protest. But a commanding voice spoke behind him.

'Let the boy alone,' said the voice.

The shopkeeper was all smiles in an instant.

'Everything is of the finest quality in my shop, sir,' he said. 'Only the best saddles and reins here, sir,' he repeated. 'The best in the whole of Anglesey.'

He tried to shoulder Caleb out of the way.

'Go away, boy,' he hissed.

But Caleb took no notice. He was gazing up

at the owner of the voice . . . and smiling. This was the kind gentleman who'd given him *two* pennies for opening the gate at Maenaddwyn. And he had his big black horse with him. Caleb longed to reach up and pat the animal's glossy neck.

'Here! Hold Prince for me,' commanded the gentleman. 'Hold him while I examine the goods in the shop.'

Caleb jumped to obey.

'At once, sir,' he said gladly.

He couldn't resist glancing over his shoulder. Maybe the shopkeeper would realise now that he wasn't just a beggar boy. Maybe he'd even offer him work!

Caleb turned back to the big black horse. He patted his neck lovingly and whispered soft words in his ear.

'There, boy,' he whispered. 'Still now, boy,' he whispered again.

The big horse stamped his hooves and nick-ered. Just as if he understood every word.

The gentleman emerged from the shop. The shopkeeper was bowing at his side.

'See that everything is ready for tomorrow,' the gentleman ordered.

'Of course, Mr Wyn,' said the shopkeeper rubbing his hands. 'Your order will be attended to at once. I shall see to it personally.'

Mr Wyn turned and smiled at Caleb.

'You can handle horses, I see,' he said, noting how Prince stayed quiet and still while Caleb held the reins.

'Oh yes!' said Caleb.

Mr Wyn walked forward to grasp the reins. Then he looked at Caleb again.

'Haven't I seen you before?' he asked.

Caleb nodded.

'Yes, sir,' he said. 'At Maenaddwyn.'

'Hm!' said Mr Wyn eyeing him thoughtfully. 'You've come to work on the mountain, I expect.'

Caleb tried to stand strong and tall, but he couldn't keep the sadness from his face.

'They won't have me,' he said.

Mr Wyn examined him from top to toe. He saw how thin and weak looking Caleb was, although he stood so proudly.

'Forget the copper,' he said. 'Try working with horses. What's your name?'

'Caleb, sir.'

'Well, remember what I've told you, Caleb,' said Mr Wyn. 'Try working with horses.'

He reached into his pocket and handed Caleb two pennies.

'For holding Prince,' he said.

He mounted and rode swiftly away.

Caleb gazed after him longingly. Then he looked at the pennies in his hand. How kind

Mr Wyn was. *Two* pennies just for holding the reins! He put them safely in his pocket.

Why didn't I ask Mr Wyn for work, Caleb thought suddenly. Maybe if he ran fast enough he could still catch him. He started down the street.

'Mr Wyn!' he called desperately as the horse and rider disappeared round the corner.

But it was no use. He couldn't run fast enough. Besides his back ached too much. He slowed to a walk as he tried to think what to do next.

Suddenly he heard shouts and hurrying feet behind him. He grasped the pennies in his pocket ... hard! A gang of children were running towards him, shouting and waving their arms excitedly.

Were they going to steal from him? He squeezed himself against the wall and prepared to fight and kick and punch to save his precious pennies. But they ran past without noticing him.

'Hurry! Hurry! The copper carts are coming!' they shouted. 'Now for a ride.'

Where there were carts there would be horses too, thought Caleb. He straightened suddenly. *That* was where he would find work. With the copper carts and their horses. He tried to ignore the pain in his back as he hurried after the children.

But he couldn't hurry fast enough. He bit his lip and tried to stop the tears that lurked behind his eyelids. A ten year old boy didn't cry. Even when the breath stabbed at his lungs, and the pain in his back made every step an agony.

There was a cloud of dust ahead and the steady rumble of cartwheels. He could hear the slow clip-clop of tired hooves and the encouraging shouts of the drivers. He could catch them yet.

He hurried on. He must reach them before they passed. Then he would be able to offer himself for work. *Any* work as long as it was with horses.

The carts appeared in a long line. The air was full of suffocating dust as the wheels lurched along the stony road. The horses strained and pulled while the men cracked their whips and shouted encouragement. Caleb ran towards them.

'Can I work with the horses?' he shouted.

'Keep away. And don't ride on the cart,' growled one of the men angrily. 'Keep away.'

'But I want to work with horses,' said Caleb.

'Away with you before I give you a taste of my whip,' shouted the man again.

He turned towards the children clutching and riding the back of the cart.

'Away!' He cracked his whip above their heads. 'Away with you!'

They scattered, laughing.

Caleb stood disconsolately as he watched the carts making their slow way down to the harbour. Now his last hope had gone. He had no choice but to go home and admit that he hadn't found work. Mam would be sympathetic. She would put her arm around his shoulders and pretend that he'd find work tomorrow, or maybe the next day. But he knew better. He hated Amlwch and the Copper Mountain.

He turned towards home clutching the two pennies tightly in his pocket. Two pennies were better than nothing, he decided. They'd buy *something*, wouldn't they? And maybe, if he was lucky, he'd earn more tomorrow.

7

Caleb was without work throughout the winter months. He searched desperately every day, but nobody wanted to employ a sickly looking boy. He offered himself at all the small shops and in the alehouse too, and he climbed the mountain again and again to plead for work. But the answer was always the same.

'Nothing for a boy like you. And don't pester us again.'

Or,

'Go away, beggar boy. We don't want you here.'

'But I'm not a beggar,' protested Caleb. 'Please! I'll do anything.'

But nobody listened. And Caleb would clutch his threadbare clothes tighter to his chest and try to forget that he was cold and hungry, and that his boots were worn through. And of course, there was no money to repair them.

'They're past repairing,' said Da shaking his head anxiously. 'They might as well be thrown away.'

'But Caleb can't walk the streets barefoot,' Mam said. 'Not without boots, John. He'll be ill with the fever again.'

Her voice was full of tears.

'Wrap straw around his feet and ankles, and tie it on with string,' advised Aunt Margaret. 'That will keep him warm.'

Mam swallowed . . . hard.

'But street children do that,' she protested. 'Beggar children.'

'Blame the stewards,' said Uncle Tomos. 'It's their fault.'

He banged his fist on the table.

'They expect us to work for a pittance, although bread is costing more. Too much rain and a bad harvest, they say. But who cares about us? We can starve for all they care. And what about that ship in the harbour? The 'Wellington'. It's full of corn. But not for the likes of us. Oh no! They'll sell it for a high price at Liverpool. That corn should be ours. Anglesey corn for Anglesey people, I say.'

Da nodded in agreement.

'Some of us,' said Uncle Tomos, 'are going to prevent that ship from sailing. Are you with us, John? And you, William?'

Caleb listened in amazement. What were they going to do? What if they were punished, and maybe sent to prison? His heart started to beat painfully.

Uncle Tomos lowered his voice and spoke very very softly. Just as if he expected somebody to be listening outside the door.

'We're going down to the harbour, John,' he whispered. 'We'll steal the ship's rudder. And then the corn will be ours.'

'Hurrah!' cheered some of the children.

'Hush!' warned Uncle Tomos.

'Can we come too?' whispered the children.

'You'll stay here. All of you,' said Aunt Margaret commandingly.

Caleb relaxed. He felt thankful, but also disappointed. He wanted to take part although he was afraid.

'Are you game?' hissed Huw in his ear.

'Game?'

'To slip out and see the fun, of course. Or are you a cry-baby?'

Caleb stiffened. Of course, he wasn't a cry-baby.

'If you go, I'll go,' he said.

'Come on, then,' whispered Huw watching his mother carefully. 'Now, while she's not looking.'

The street was full of people shoving and pushing and shouting. They were on their way to the harbour.

'Food for our children,' they shouted angrily.

'Down with the stewards.'

'A fair wage for a fair day's work.'

'Anglesey corn for Anglesey people.'

The voices echoed around the street.

'Don't let our Da's see us,' said Huw. 'They'd send us home, and we'd miss the fun.'

The voices were raised again.

'To the harbour.'

'Stop the 'Wellington'.'

'It's our corn.'

Caleb and Huw started shouting too. They waved their fists and stamped their feet in time with the crowd. Caleb forgot about the straw tied around his feet and ankles. It didn't matter that he was poor and hungry and dressed in rags. He was part of the crowd. A

50

determined crowd that was going to see justice done.

He watched as Da and Uncle Tomos boarded the 'Wellington'. They were met by a line of sailors. Would there be a fight? Suddenly Caleb felt very frightened. What if Da was killed?

'The sailors won't fight,' shouted Huw. 'See, they're frightened. Our men will win.'

Caleb smiled thankfully.

'Look. They've got the rudder,' shouted Huw. 'Come on. They're carrying it to the town.'

'But what will happen now?' asked Caleb.

'Who cares?' said Huw. 'The "Wellington" can't sail. We've won.'

The crowd shouted triumphantly as the rudder was carried shoulder high towards the town. Huw clutched Caleb's arm and pulled him along.

'Wait,' said Caleb. 'Where are they taking it?'

'To the cemetery,' said Huw. 'Maybe there'll be some real fighting soon.'

But Caleb had had enough. He pulled back and shook his head determinedly.

'I'm going home,' he said. 'Mam will be worried.'

'Baby!'

But Caleb didn't care what Huw called him. He was cold and tired, and his back ached again. He walked away slowly, ignoring the rowdy groups that stood yelling on the street. But suddenly their voices rose threatingly, and they began running towards the top of the street.

'There's one of them.'

'Corn for Liverpool, and money in his pocket.'

'*He's* not starving.'

Caleb hesitated. What was happening? He stood on tiptoe and tried to see better. But he was so small amongst the crowd. Somebody was riding up the street. Who? The crowd pushed forward.

'Look at him.'

'He's rich, while we starve.'

'Pull him from his horse.'

Caleb caught his breath suddenly. *Who was the rider*? Not ... not ... Mr Wyn? His Mr Wyn? No. No. Of course, not. Hadn't he searched and searched for him all through the long winter months.

He had to make sure. But how? Then he spotted a water barrel by the wall. If he climbed on top, he would be able to see better.

'Stop him.'

'Pull him from his horse.'

The shouting grew louder as he struggled to climb the barrel. He slipped. He bit his lip as

the pain shot through his back. But he had to see. He climbed again and tried to balance on the narrow lip.

It was Mr Wyn! His Mr Wyn, and he was in danger. Terrible danger. He must be saved at once. And it was up to him, Caleb.

He tried to jump from the barrel. But in his haste he lost his balance. He was slipping . . . slipping into the barrel. He tried to save himself by clutching at the wall. But his nails scraped painfully along the rough stones until the blood flowed. He fell up to his waist into the cold, cold water.

But there was no time to lose. Even though his teeth were chattering and his fingers hurt so much. He must climb out somehow and rush to save Mr Wyn.

The wet straw hung limply from his feet and ankles as he rushed forward, and tried to squeeze himself through the crowd.

'Keep your shoving to yourself, you,' threatened a man savagely.

But Caleb took no notice. He had to reach Mr Wyn.

'Leave him alone,' he shouted. 'It's Mr Wyn.'

But nobody heard. They were too busy shouting and shaking their fists and threatening. Mr Wyn and Prince were surrounded.

'No. No. Don't!' shouted Caleb as he tried to push through the crowd again.

Mr Wyn fought to control Prince. But the horse was frightened. He danced nervously and threw his head up wildly. The crowd scattered a little. They were afraid of the dancing hooves.

Then a man jumped forward and jerked Mr Wyn from the saddle.

'No!' shouted Caleb as Mr Wyn fell and cracked his head on the stony street.

Prince neighed loudly. His head shot up and his eyes rolled in fright. Then there was a clatter of hooves as he galloped away.

The crowd formed a threatening circle around Mr Wyn's fallen body.

'Serves him right,' growled a man.

'Yes! Yes!' shouted the crowd.

Some raised their clubs to strike.

Caleb rushed through. He stood protectively over Mr Wyn.

'It's Mr Wyn,' he cried. 'He's a kind man.'

'Kind?' laughed the crowd. 'None of the rich are kind. They sell their corn, and starve the poor.'

'No,' said Caleb. 'Mr Wyn would never do that.'

He stood there daring the crowd to lift a finger.

Suddenly somebody laughed.

'Look at him. Little bulldog.'

'What will you do to us?' laughed another. 'Bite us?'

'There's better fun to be had,' a voice called. 'He's a brave boy. Leave him and his kind gentleman. To the cemetery, lads.'

Soon they were all gone.

'Mr Wyn! Mr Wyn!'

Caleb bent over the still body. Would the crowd return? And would they really hurt Mr Wyn this time? Then Mr Wyn's eyes opened slowly. He struggled to sit up and look about him.

'My horse,' he said. 'Where's Prince?'

'He ran away, Mr Wyn,' said Caleb. 'Can you get up? Lean on me, Mr Wyn.'

Mr Wyn looked at him again.

'Why . . . it's Caleb,' he said. 'The boy who likes horses.'

He leaned shakily against the wall and took a large white handkerchief from his pocket. He tried to staunch the blood running down his cheek.

Caleb was worried when he saw so much blood.

'Are you all right, sir?'

'Yes . . . thanks to you,' said Mr Wyn.

He tried to walk a little but his legs wouldn't support him.

'Lean on me,' said Caleb. 'I'll take you home. Mam and Aunt Margaret will look after you.'

It would be cold and damp in the cottage, and the fire would be low in the hearth. But Mr Wyn would be safe from the crowd there.

8

Da and Uncle Tomos had just returned from the cemetery. They were excited as they related the happenings to Mam and Aunt Margaret. How they had stormed aboard the 'Wellington' and taken the rudder. And how they'd carried it shoulder high to the cemetery.

'Now the "Wellington" can't sail,' said Uncle Tomos. 'There'll be enough corn for everybody.'

Then Huw told them that Caleb was missing.

'He started home long ago,' he said. 'By himself.'

'Why didn't you stop him?' said Mam. 'You know he's not strong.'

She turned anxiously to Da.

'What could have happened to him?' she asked.

Then the door opened and Caleb and Mr Wyn staggered in. The family stared open-mouthed.

'Mr Wyn has been hurt,' said Caleb.

Nobody moved.

'Man hurt,' said Catrin. She started to cry. 'There's blood. Lots of blood. Catrin's afraid of blood.'

Mam held her tight while her eyes held Da's. Nobody moved.

Mr Wyn collapsed on to the bench and rested his head on the damp wall. He looked pale and ill.

'Will you have a drink of water?' said Uncle Tomos at last.

He sounded angry.

'We workers have nothing else to offer you,' he added. 'Not even a spare crust.'

'It isn't Mr Wyn's fault,' said Caleb quickly. 'He's kind. He gave me two pennies in Maen-addwyn, and two more for holding his horse in Amlwch.'

'And what is he doing here? Is he a Justice of the Peace?' asked Uncle Tomos angrily.

Mr Wyn listened quietly as he looked around the cottage.

'I'm Mr Wyn, Squire of Tremarchog,' he said at last. 'I'm not here to arrest anybody, whatever acts they've committed.'

'Let me see your wound.'

Aunt Margaret bustled forward with warm water and a rag to wash away the blood. Then she told Mr Wyn to sit and rest quietly.

Nobody spoke for a long time. They all watched Mr Wyn as he rested with eyes closed.

58

Slowly the colour returned to his face. At last, he opened his eyes.

'Caleb saved me from the mob,' he said.

He put a hand in his pocket.

'I would like to give you money for your kindness. You could buy bread for the children.'

Uncle Tomos drew himself up proudly.

'We're not begging,' he said. 'A proper wage is all we ask, and a fair price to pay for our bread.'

But he couldn't help staring at the money Mr Wyn offered. It was a whole month's wage, maybe more.

Caleb had been standing quietly. He was so glad that Squire Wyn was better and that the colour had returned to his cheeks. He knew that soon he would get up and leave the cottage. And maybe he'd never see him again. He knew he must ask him for work. *Now!*

He tried to stand straight and tall as he stepped forward.

'Mr Wyn,' he said. He swallowed nervously. '*Squire* Wyn,' he said again. 'I want work more than anything. I've looked and looked, but there's no work to be had. I want to work with horses, Mr Wyn. Please have you work for me? Please!'

'Caleb!' warned Da.

Squire Wyn looked hard at Caleb. He saw how thin and tired he was, and that he held himself as if his back was painful. But he also saw how determined Caleb looked, and he remembered that Caleb had saved him from the mob.

'And that's what you want, Caleb, is it?' he asked. 'To work for me?'

'Oh yes, sir,' said Caleb.

The Squire turned to Uncle Tomos.

'Do you want to work for me too?' he asked. 'Do you want to leave Amlwch?'

'We work the copper,' said Uncle Tomos stiffly. 'And Margaret is a Copper Lady.'

'But you need money to buy bread,' said Squire Wyn putting coins on the table.

'We'd never beg,' said Uncle Tomos proudly.

But he accepted the money.

'And what about you?' said Mr Wyn looking at Mam and Da. 'Are you settled here at Amlwch?'

Da hesitated. Then he shook his head.

'We're country people,' he said. 'And we're used to country ways. But we've no choice. We must go where there's work to be had.'

Squire Wyn rubbed his chin thoughfully.

'I have an empty cottage on the estate,' he said finally. 'There will be work for Caleb in the stables, and for you somewhere on the estate. I have a debt to pay. Because Caleb saved me from the mob. If he hadn't, who knows what might have happened?'

Da hesitated. Would they be happy at Tremarchog? He looked at Mam. He saw that there was hope on her face.

Caleb kept his eyes on Da. Surely he wasn't going to refuse? Not when they could leave Amlwch for ever, and live in the country once again. How he longed to go back. He wanted to hear the birds sing in spring and to watch the lambs frolicking in the fields. He wanted to pick blackberries and enjoy sunshine free from the smoke and stench of Amlwch. And he wanted to work with horses. With the Squire's horses. Fine horses like Prince, with tossing manes and shiny coats and dancing hooves. He crossed his fingers and prayed.

'You go, John,' said Uncle Tomos. 'We're settled here in Amlwch. But, you go.'

What would Da decide? Caleb could hardly breathe as he waited. Then he saw the smile on Da's face as he nodded.

'Thank you, sir,' said Da. 'We'll be happy to accept.'

Caleb smiled at Huw.

'I have work now,' he said proudly. 'With horses.'